Sir Gawain and the Rugby Sevens

KU-225-164

Contents

For Simon Eaves and
Grant Wilkinson.

Chapter 1

THE BIGGEST KNIGHT IN CAMELOT

In the days of good King Arthur there were lots of knights who were very good at fighting.

There was Sir Lancelot, who was never *ever* beaten at a joust.

GOWAR, Mick

Comets: Sir Gawain and the rugby sevens

Please return/renew this item by the last
date shown

CCTA LIBRARIES LLYFRGELLAU CCTA

Collins Educational
An imprint of **HarperCollins***Publishers*

Published by Collins Educational
77-85 Fulham Palace Road, London W6 8JB.

© HarperCollins*Publishers*

ISBN 0 00 323048 1

Mick Gowar asserts the moral right to be identified as
the author of this work.

Reprinted 1996

Illustration and page layout by Clinton Banbury
Cover design and illustration by Clinton Banbury

Commissioning Editor: Domenica de Rosa
Editors: Rebecca Lloyd and Paula Hammond
Production: Mandy Inness

Typeset by Quintessence, Billericay.
Printed by HarperCollinsManufacturing Glasgow

There were the twins, Sir Balin and Sir Balan. No one –
not even Merlin – could tell them apart. They always
fought together on the same side, and this confused the
other knights terribly, especially Sir Bors.

There was Sir Bedevere, probably the most intelligent knight. There was Sir Percival, a gentle knight, who wasn't that keen on fighting anyway. And there was Sir Kay, who was quite simply a coward.

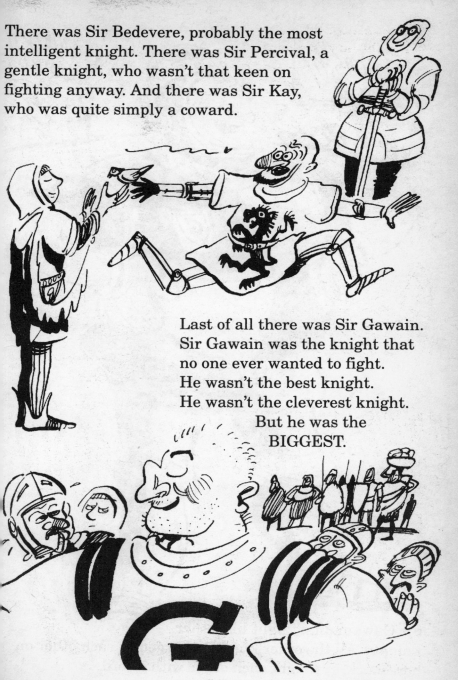

Last of all there was Sir Gawain. Sir Gawain was the knight that no one ever wanted to fight. He wasn't the best knight. He wasn't the cleverest knight. But he was the BIGGEST.

Sir Gawain didn't fight like other
knights. All the other knights charged at each other on
horseback, or fought each other with swords.

6

Sir Gawain hardly ever rode a horse.

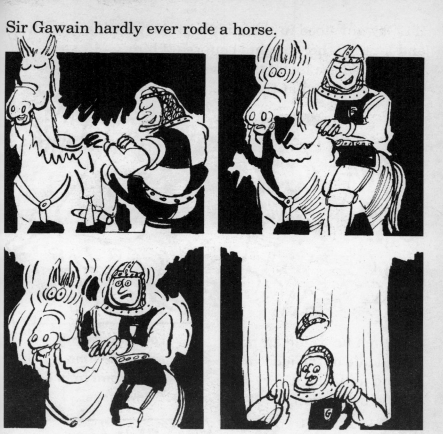

Even the biggest horses sagged in the middle when Sir Gawain tried to mount them.

Sir Gawain didn't fight with a sword. His father had always told him that fencing was for sissies.

Fencing is for sissies, son.

Sir Gawain stood in the middle of the jousting ground and let the other knights bounce off him.
Then he fell on top of them with an enormous crash.
Then he laughed at them.

And then he would stand in the middle of the jousting ground and sing a very rude song which began:

His mother had sung it to him when he was a baby.

The song made all Queen Guinevere's ladies-in-waiting blush.

The knights didn't mind the song. They didn't really mind the laughing. What they *hated* was being beaten by Sir Gawain.

Chapter 2
PLOTTING AGAINST SIR GAWAIN

One day Sir Gawain
was out being fitted for
a new suit of armour.

So all the other knights
decided to have a special
meeting.

11

Sir Lancelot, you're the jousting champion. You do it!

GULP!

Um... well... normally I would. But I've got this terrible cold

And it seems to have got worse since, erm, since Sir Gawain fell on me.

COUGH! COUGH!

COUGH!! COUGH!!

And Sir Lancelot coughed twice more to make sure that everybody understood that if it hadn't been for his cold – and the sun in his eyes – he would have beaten Sir Gawain easily.

GHA NGHA HANGHA HA HA

A peculiar gargling noise came from inside Sir Bors's bandages.

King Arthur was in his Counting House with Merlin. They had just finished counting.

Well, Sire, you do have a lot of knights to feed.

But this isn't the food for all the knights! That's what Sir Gawain gets through on his own!

He is a growing knight, Your Majesty.

King Arthur shuddered at the thought of Gawain growing any bigger.

He told me he was 'in training', Sire.

The King shuddered again.

What for?

14

They were interruped by a shout from outside.

No, I don't think so...

He's an old friend of your half-sister, Morgan Le Fay.

If he's a friend of Morgan's he can't be very nice.

Precisely!

Are you sure this is a good idea?

Trust me, Your Majesty. Just trust me...

Merlin knew the Green Knight would be a good match for Sir Gawain, so he set about finding him.

Now Merlin had the Green Knight's address, but he didn't write him a letter. He sent him a message by magic. Far away in South London, the Green Knight received the message, but, by some strange quirk of magic, he thought it was from his mate Dave.

Chapter 3

THE GREEN KNIGHT

Queen Guinevere looked around the hall. She smiled at King Arthur. She kissed him on the cheek.

This is lovely! A proper dinner party! So much nicer than those horrid, rough tournaments and jousts. This is what knights should do, not all that nasty fighting!

All King Arthur's knights were sitting at the Round Table. They were wearing their best armour. All the ladies-in-waiting were wearing their prettiest dresses. In the centre of the table was a big vase of spring flowers. Each knight had his own napkin with his own coat of arms sewn on it. In front of each guest was a tiny glass half-filled with little shreds of lettuce and a pink, gloopy mixture.

19

Everyone looked happy –
except Sir Gawain.

King Arthur flinched.

Sir Gawain stared down at his half glass of pink gloop in disbelief.

But, Boss, if this is the food, where are the chips?

This is Prawn Cocktail. It will be followed by chicken salad. There's Black Forest Cake for afters. AND THERE ARE NO CHIPS!

Suddenly the door burst open. Into the hall galloped an enormous man riding a gigantic horse.

They were both bright green from head to foot (or from nose to tail).

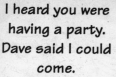
I heard you were having a party. Dave said I could come.

This is a private party. Erm... we don't have enough food or drink for anyone else.

No sweat! I've had a take-away. And I've brought some drink with me.

erm...

...well...

FUMBLE...

where is it?

AH!

'ere you go!

CAMELOT SPECIAL BREW

23

The Knights of the Round Table looked terrified. Sir Lancelot started coughing, very loudly.

YOU HEARD THE BOSS— ON YOUR BIKE!

All the knights and ladies looked round. Sir Gawain was marching across the room. He was rolling up the sleeves of his chain-mail shirt. He looked *very* mean.

The Green Knight and Sir Gawain stood toe to toe, and eyeball to eyeball. Then they drew apart.

The other knights flinched, but both Gawain and the Green Knight remained standing. The Green Knight really *was* a match for Sir Gawain.

27

Two hours later, Sir Gawain and the Green Knight were *still* trying to knock seven bells out of each other.

Sir Gawain and the Green Knight looked around the
Great Hall. They were all alone. In fact, everyone else
had got fed up and gone to bed ages ago. But the Green
Knight and Sir Gawain had been enjoying themselves so
much they hadn't noticed.

Boring lot, your mates.

I know.

Why don't you come back to my place? I've got some great mates and we have brilliant fun!

There's the Red Knight, and the Black Knight, and the Blue Knight, and the Yellow Knight and the...

...Grey Knight with Purple Stripes! And we've invented this new way of fighting – you'd love it!

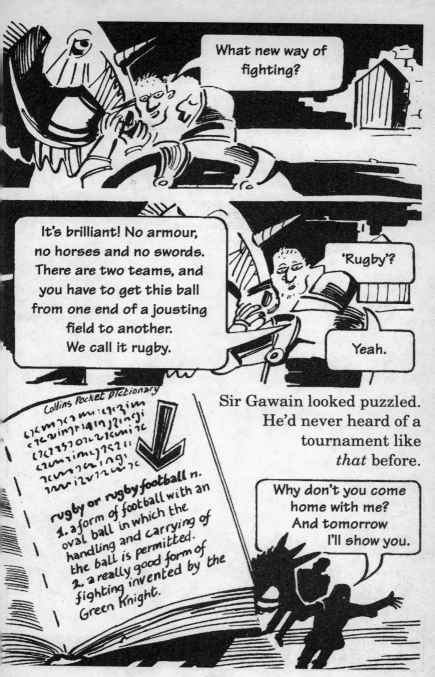

A few minutes later, the sentry at the gate saw two enormous men, one of them bright green, marching towards him with their arms round each other's shoulders. Behind them trotted an enormous green horse.

The Green Knight and Sir Gawain left Camelot with the green horse trotting calmly behind them.

Chapter 4

THE CHALLENGE

Two weeks later a letter arrived
at Camelot.
It was addressed to King Arthur
and written on bright
green paper.
The king read the letter,
then he called for Merlin.

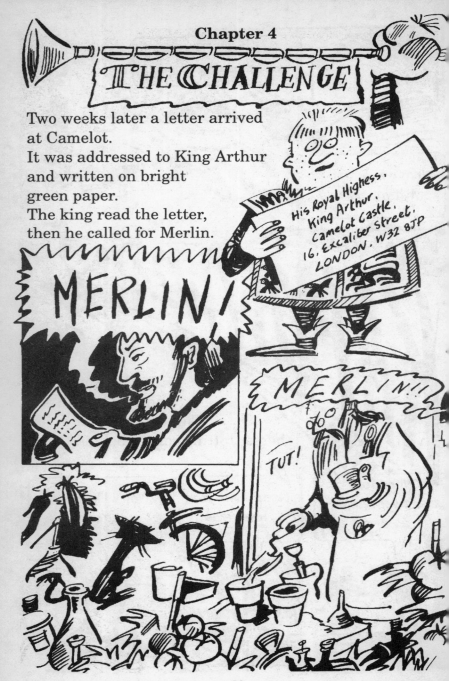

His Royal Highess,
King Arthur,
Camelot Castle,
16, Excaliber Street,
LONDON. W32 8JP

MERLIN!

MERLIN!!

TUT!

King Arthur handed the green
letter to Merlin.

Dear King Arthur,
Sir Gawain and the Green Knight
(and the Red Knight and the Black
Knight and the Blue Knight and the
Yellow Knight and the Grey Knight
with Purple Stripes) challenge the
Knights of the Round Table to a
tournament.
Meet us next Saturday at the
jousting field of Twickenham.
Seven-a-side. No horses, swords
or armour allowed. No magic
(that means YOU Merlin).
Your obedient subjects,
Green, RED, Black, BLUE, YELLOW, Grey with
Purple Stripes and GAWAIN (Knights).
P.S. Bring a bottle.

COUGH!
COUGH!

Oh, dear.
I don't like the look of
this one bit.

King Arthur and Merlin were sitting in the Royal Box, gazing down on the tournament field at Twickenham. Below them, fourteen men were getting ready to do battle.

To the right of the Royal Box was Sir Gawain and the Green Knight's 'Barbarians' team. They were enormous men with broken noses, cauliflower ears, chipped teeth and huge muscles.
In fact they all looked a bit like Sir Gawain.

They were glaring at the Camelot team who were facing them across the muddy field.

The Camelot team were... well, looking rather unhappy.

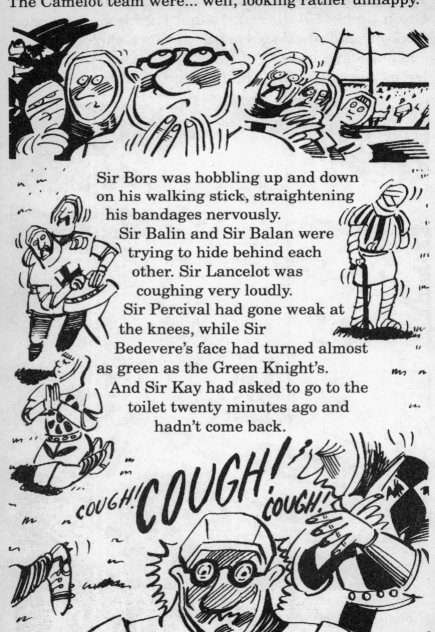

Sir Bors was hobbling up and down on his walking stick, straightening his bandages nervously.

Sir Balin and Sir Balan were trying to hide behind each other. Sir Lancelot was coughing very loudly.

Sir Percival had gone weak at the knees, while Sir Bedevere's face had turned almost as green as the Green Knight's.

And Sir Kay had asked to go to the toilet twenty minutes ago and hadn't come back.

COUGH! COUGH! COUGH!

The Royal Herald blew a fanfare on his trumpet.

An expectant hush settled over the crowd of spectators

The New Tournament is about to begin. Here are the rules.

Rules of Rugby

1

The team which can carry the ball into their opponents' half of the field and put it down behind their opponents' flagpole the most times will be the winner.

2.

No swords, horses - or magic allowed.

Then King Arthur went down to the field to supervise the toss.

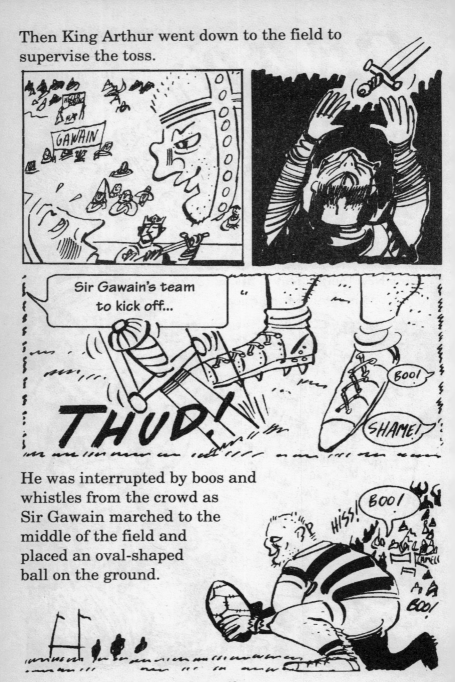

He was interrupted by boos and whistles from the crowd as Sir Gawain marched to the middle of the field and placed an oval-shaped ball on the ground.

Sir Gawain gave the ball an enormous kick.

The Camelot team watched as the ball became a distant speck, then slowly began to fall back to earth.

44

Sir Bors didn't have time to say anything else, as seven enormous men with cauliflower ears and broken teeth all jumped on him at once.

Chapter 5

MERLIN'S PLAN

King Arthur and Merlin sat alone in the Royal Box.
The Tournament was over. The crowd had all gone home.

All that remained of the great battle were the discarded
chip wrappers and empty cans of *Camelot Special Brew*
that littered the ground.

But I do have some good news, too.

What's that?

Well, your majesty, after the Tournament I went to see Sir Gawain and the Green Knight. I told them how well they had done.

I said you were very, very pleased with their New Tournament idea.

YOU DID WHAT?

So tomorrow Sir Gawain and the Green Knight set off for Wales, then Scotland, then Ireland. After that, I thought they could go to France.

France?

New Zealand?

ER, HUM!

Then I suggested they might go to a small country I've heard of, on the other side of the world. It's called New Zealand.

A WORLD ATLAS

Thanks.

NEW ZEALAND IS 12,000 MILES FROM BRITAIN.

But that does mean that we'll need a new knight to replace Sir Gawain. And I don't want any more thugs.

I've been thinking about what Queen Guinevere said. Knights should be more than just hooligans on horseback.

I've already thought of that, Your Majesty. My third cousin's youngest sister's uncle's godson should do nicely.

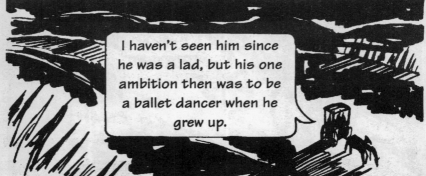

I haven't seen him since he was a lad, but his one ambition then was to be a ballet dancer when he grew up.

53

Chapter 6

THE NEW KNIGHT

King Arthur and Merlin were in the Counting House. King Arthur was doing some very complicated sums – with Merlin's help, of course.

With the money we save on Sir Gawain's food, we'll be able to buy a napkin ring for every knight...

...and have enough to buy net curtains for the dungeons. Queen Guinevere's very keen on net curtains. We might also have enough money for some of those furry lid covers for the toilets...

He was interrupted by a knock on the door.

KNOCK! KNOCK!

TOOT to TOOT!!

Sir Botham of Headingley to see his majesty.

Who?

It's my third cousin's youngest sister's uncle's godson. The one I told you about.

Yes, of course. Send him in, herald.

55

But before the herald could move, the door burst open and in marched an enormous, muscular man carrying a long bag.

King Arthur and Merlin both went pale. Sir Botham looked just like Sir Gawain – only bigger!

Sir Botham opened his bag and pulled out a long
wooden club and a small cannon ball that had been
painted bright red.

59

King Arthur buried his head in his hands.

Merlin patted the
king on the back.

Oh, no! Not again!

Don't worry,
Your Majesty.
It'll never catch on...